friendly ph

MW01716023

Rainy Day Play

By Cindy Leaney

Illustrated by Sue King and Peter Wilks

ROURKE CLASSROOM RESOURCES

The path to student success

Note to Parents and Teachers/Educators

Before reading: Ask your child what this book might be about. Then ask what part of *rainy*, *day* and *play* sounds the same. Then ask what sound *a* in *cat* makes. Is it the same or different? Remind your child to listen for those sounds in the story.

Written by Cindy Leaney
Designed by Ruth Shane
Illustrated by Sue King & Peter Wilks
Project managed by Gemma Cooper

Created and Designed by SGA and Media Management
18 High Street, Hadleigh, Suffolk, IP7 5AP, U.K.

P.O. Box 3328, Vero Beach
Florida, 32964, U.S.A.
Editor: Patty Whitehouse

Printed in China

ISBN 1-58952-899-9

Rainy Day Play

Rain, rain, go away.
Come again another day!

It is a gray, rainy day.

But don't be sad! We can put on a play!

A play? Okay!

We can pretend we are in castles and fantastic places!

We can wear capes and hats

and paint our faces!

I've always wanted to be in a play.

What do you say?
May I act in your play?

But you are a cat. What about that?

Cats can act. They're good, in fact.

Okay, okay, we can all act in the play.

Let's make up a story and

something to say.

One day, in a castle faraway…
some children saw a magic cat!

The cat gave them a magic map and
a big black hat.

"Put on the hat, put your finger on the map.

You can go anywhere at all,
just like that."

Okay! Hooray!

That's a fantastic rainy day play.

Game time!

Match the words and pictures.

1. castle
2. cape
3. map
4. hat
5. rain

a

b

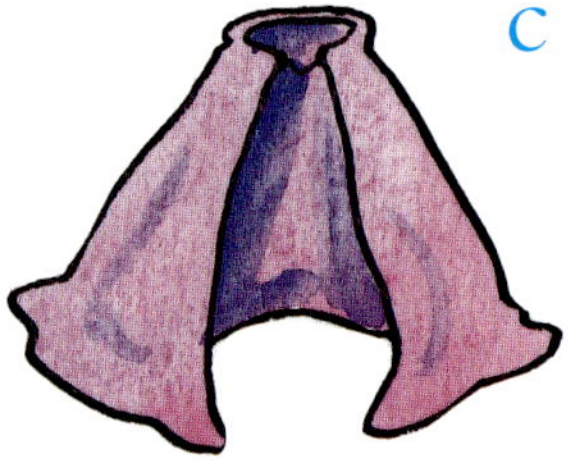

c

d

e

Answers: **1.** b, **2.** c, **3.** e, **4.** a, **5.** d.

In the word *cape a* says its name.

In which of these words does *a* say its name?

castle day fantastic game map
okay play rain

Answers: day, game, okay, play, rain.